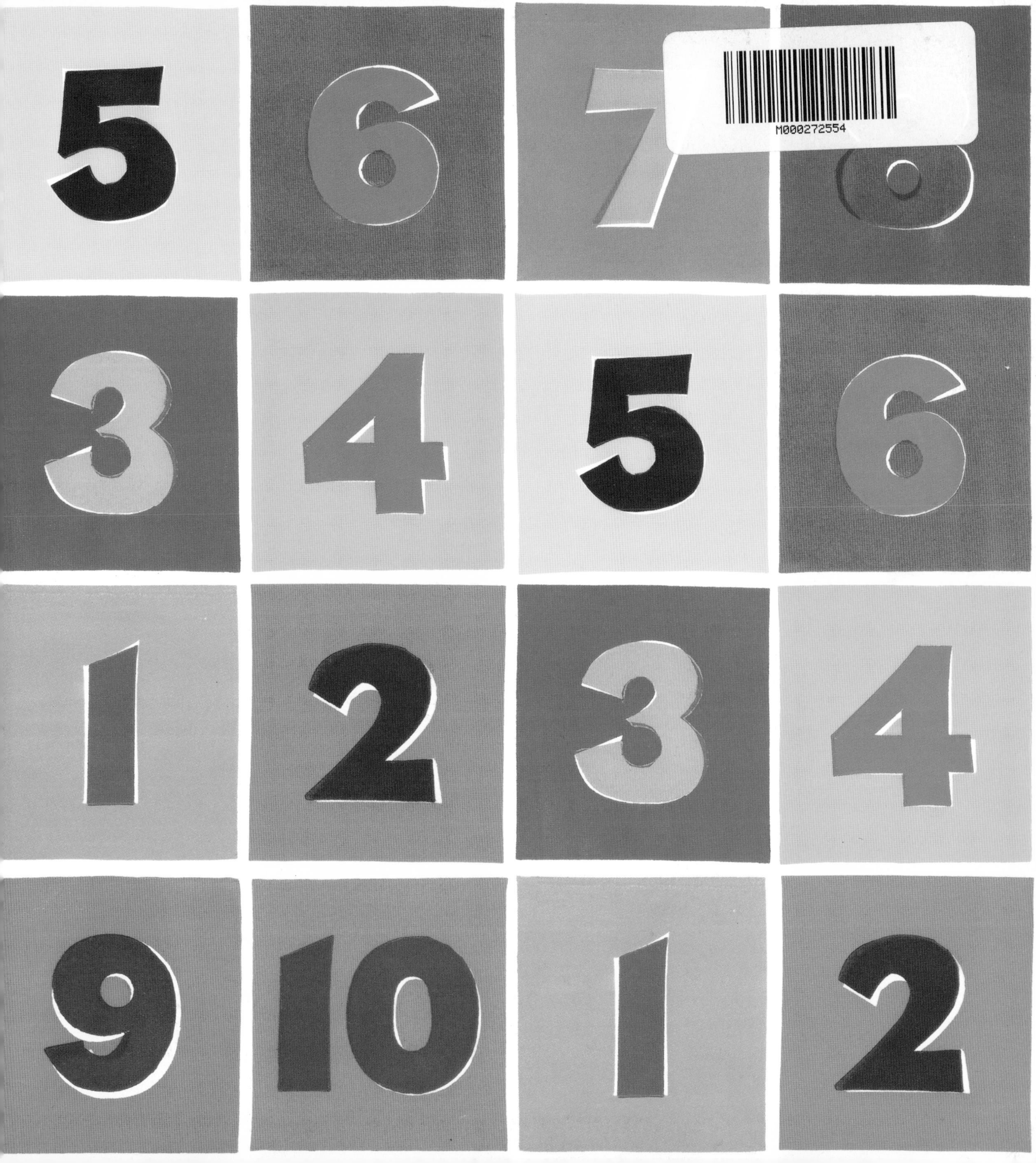
5 6 7 8
3 4 5 6
1 2 3 4
9 10 1 2

Hide & Seek

Janet S. Wong

PICTURES BY Margaret Chodos-Irvine

HARCOURT, INC. Orlando Austin New York San Diego Toronto London

PRINTED IN SINGAPORE

Cookie time
is the perfect time

for hide-and-seek.

Dad,
don't peek!

1

ONE

Hide-and-seek means
find a fat tree,

stand behind it
tall and thin,

don't scratch,

don't sneeze —

hide
and freeze.

2

TWO

Hide-and-seek means
squeeze yourself small,

roll yourself tight
into a ball,

make yourself soft
like jelly-jam mush,

don't dig a hole
in the ground now—

hush.

THREE

Hide-and-seek means
open a box,

slide inside,

close the top,

hope that no one mails you away....

4

FOUR

**Hide *doesn't* mean
hide the whole day.**

5

FIVE

No,
not the trash can—

you want to stink?

6

SIX

It might be okay
to hide
under the sink

with a bathtub pail
and a boat
and a whale

as long as you hide
that curly dog tail.

7

SEVEN

Who put the bubble gum
under the desk?

EIGHT

How about a lampshade on your head?

9

NINE

**What if we hide under the covers,
under the pillows
in the great big bed?**

10

TEN!

READY OR NOT,

HERE I COME!

When we're ready to be found,

we snap our fingers,
clap our hands,

sing a sound like
ahumm-hurrumpf
or
wooooooodelloooooo!

But...
shhhhhhh...
we're not ready yet.

When the oven bell rings
and the cookies are done,

that's when
to end
the hide-and-seek fun.

Bing!

**Now's the time
to creep down the hall.**

**Stand
behind
the kitchen
wall.**

Peek,
sneak out.

Then jump
and shout,

"Here I am!"

For Andrew, my hide-and-seek buddy—J. S. W.

For Peter —M. C.-I.

www.HarcourtBooks.com

Library of Congress Cataloging-in-Publication Data
Wong, Janet S.
Hide & seek/Janet S. Wong; illustrated by Margaret Chodos-Irvine.
p. cm.
Summary: In this counting book, a child and parent play hide-and-seek
while they bake cookies. [1. Hide and seek—Fiction. 2. Stories in rhyme.
3. Counting.] I. Title: Hide & seek.
II. Chodos-Irvine, Margaret, ill. III. Title.
PZ8.3.W8465Hid 2005
[E]—dc22 2003027737
ISBN 0-15-204934-7

First edition
G F E D C B A

The illustrations in this book were created using a variety
of printmaking techniques on Rives paper.
The display type was created by Margaret Chodos-Irvine.
The text type was set in MetaPlus Bold.
Color separations by Bright Arts Ltd., Hong Kong
Printed and bound by Tien Wah Press, Singapore
This book was printed on totally chlorine-free Stora Enso Matte paper.
Production supervision by Pascha Gerlinger
Designed by Judythe Sieck

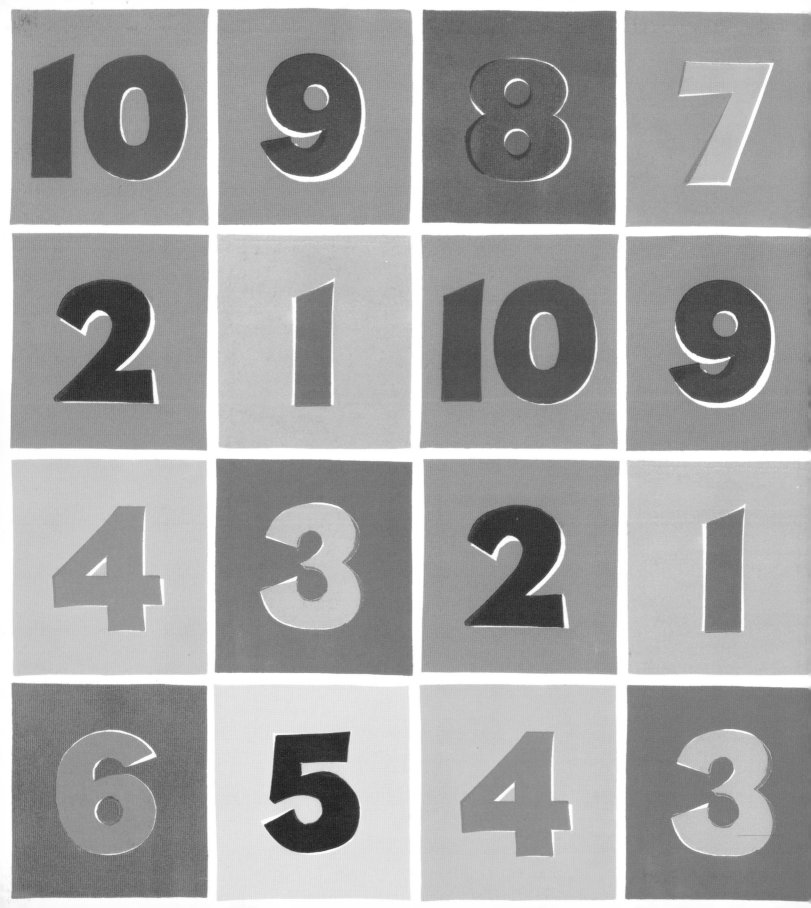